Reflections
Of Faith
and Life

Joyce Kirkby

I have a dream

You're dressing up the Christmas tree

This building

Does God live in the sky?

Life Poems

I love to watch the clouds
Another summer day
April Fool's day
Christmas at Grandad's
Esmeralda
Garrowby hill
Fond memories
Mum's visit
My dining room
The doors are always open
The beauty of nature

Heads held low

Heads held low
At the break of dawn
The Saviour gone
What else to do but mourn
Then suddenly they see
A glorious light
An angel so lovely
All dressed in white
Why do you seek Him
Among the dead?
He's risen you see
The angel said
The tomb lay empty
Their hearts leapt with joy
They couldn't wait To share the story
Same women
Same day
The difference was
The stone rolled away.

Run To You

I run to you Lord as waves rush to the shore
I want to know your word, I want to love you more
I want to know your heart, feel how it breaks
I need a new start no matter what it takes
If I humble myself, become more loke you,
your patient and kind in all that you do
If I listen to you and all that you say, then I'll follow
you and I won't go astray

No room at the Inn

No room at the inn, they say
Instead a manger filled with hay
No royal robes for this baby King
Still, hark the herald angels sing
3 wise men visit from afar
Following the shining star
Gold, frankincense, and myrrh they bring
As gifts in worship of this King
Shepherds watching flocks by night
Marvel at an awesome sight
A throng of angels fills the sky
Heavenly singing from on high
Hosanna! They cry as He rides into town
Seated on a donkey, but still no royal crown
Palm leaves line the dusty streets
As people rush, the King to greet
Now crucify! They cry
His body racked and torn
The king now has a crown
But it's a crown of thorns.
Was I in that crowd, that shouted so loud?
Did I hammer the nails
In the body now frail?

For so long

For so long I rejected
His love, stayed disconnected
Till I fell at his feet
Accepted love so complete
Now truly forgiven
I call him my friend
In all situations
On Him I depend
Such mercy and grace
He gives me each day
He helps me and guides me
In all of His ways.

<u>Shepherd</u>

He's with us in joy, and with us in sadness
He feels our pain, shares our gladness
When we feel down,
He holds our hand
There's nothing he doesn't understand
His promises
He'll always keep
He's even watching while we sleep
He's counted the number of hairs on our head
And he supplies our daily bread
Our shepherd leads us day by day
His word will guide us all the way
His spirit gives us strength to face
The trials of life, and run the race.

<u>The eyes of the Father</u>

The eyes of the Father
look into every heart,
he sees all the hopelessness
that tears you apart
But if you reach out to him,
he will give you a new start,
he will heal all your hurt and pain,
he will come into your heart
The eyes of the Father
look down on you with love,
yes he sent his Son for you,
from heaven above.
Sent him to live among
folks like you and me,
sent him to die
on Calvary's tree
The eyes of the Father
look into every heart,
he is looking for a people who will set
themselves apart,
set themselves apart
to walk with him each day,
to call him "Abba Father",
as they walk in his ways

The Father's arms are open wide

The Father's arms are open wide
You'll see a welcome in His eyes
From you His face He will not hide
He will not scold or criticise
The best robe waits for you to wear
Yes those around will stop and stare
You once were lost but now you're found
You're welcome here on holy ground
Those Pharisees will not believe
That one so lost he will receive
Once clothed in rags of guilt and shame
Now cleansed, forgiven, called by name
He doesn't see your sins in Christ
His was the perfect sacrifice
His blood can make the foulest clean
In robes of righteousness you're seen

What Do You See

What do you see, when you look at me?
A Woman of faith?
A Woman of valour?
Or a Woman who cowers with fear, in the
corner
When the enemy comes, do I reach for my
sword?
Or do I run unaware of God's word?
A child Of God?
A royal princess?
Daughter of the King?
Or life in a mess?
Righteousness of Christ?
Holy and Pure, due to his finished work
Am I really sure?
Blessed beyond measure
Precious in his sight
Rejoicing in his finish work
Or striving in my own might?
Will my life make a difference?
Will I leave a mark?
Faith needs ACTIONS,
not just TALK
Will I leave a lasting legacy?
Will I be remembered?
Or pass into obscurity?

Woman at the Well

Woman at the well
What stories can you tell?
Of the day that Jesus came
Things will never be the same
Your life was dry and dead
Please tell me what He said
When He asked you for a drink
Whatever did you think?
He didn't have a jar
Though He had travelled far
You lived your life in shame
Did you think He was insane?
To speak to one like you
Can it be really true?
An offer of new life
Instead of pain and strife
Messiah really here
To wipe away each tear
Your life has purpose new
To share a love so true

I love the autumn leaves

I love the autumn leaves
But not the mess they make
Strewn across the lawn
Out comes the garden rake!
The morning's turning chilly
I need my hat and gloves
And not a single sign
Of the flowers that I love
In their place are berries
In hues of black and red
The birds will not go hungry
They will be well fed
As I walk across the field
I watch the changing seasons
I'm thankful for creation
For so many reasons beyond imagination
Changing colours to behold
It can't be a coincidence
These leaves of brown and gold
Fashioned with such care
Every tree and leaf
To everything a purpose
It's quite beyond belief
Design not evolution
Is really plain to see
Not by chance but planned
Not just them but me

You see me

You see me when I'm counting sheep
You see me when I'm fast asleep
No matter whether day or night
I'm always precious in your sight
If I should rise up with the wings of dawn
Or settle when the day is done
Or to the other end of the earth
You knew me even before my birth
In my mother's womb you formed
One you loved before I was born
Fearfully and wonderfully made
I should never be afraid
Of folks who think that I am strange
You've knit me together, me you arranged
Unique creation, created with pleasure
I'll always be your special treasure

Lighthouse

The lighthouse shines her light around
No ship here will run to ground
Warning them that rocks are near
Sailors now will have no fear
Waves are pounding on the shore
The lighthouse doesn't move, for sure
A lonely figure some would say
But it has stayed there many a day
Those rocks that once inspired fear
By light illuminated, clear
The lighthouse proudly guides the way
For many vessels every day
In this a lesson to be found
To build our lives on solid ground
To follow Jesus every day
His light will shine to show the way

Everything's changing

Everything's changing, nothing's the same
How am I supposed to stay in the game?
Things once so certain, now not so sure
The world's motives twisted instead of pure
Sin came in and spoiled the world
Now there are questions whether boy or
girl
An answer was found, a Saviour true
He took the sin of me and you
Ever unchanging, my Jesus, my friend
He's the one on whom I can depend

When adversity comes
And trouble seems dire
Don't make the mistake
Of being stuck in the mire

Just open the pages
Of the Bible, you'll find
A living word
Will calm your mind

For every situation
There's an answer to be found
Words of wisdom
When problems abound

It's sharper than a sword
A weapon in your hand
On that you can rely on
It's there upon demand

Meditate and ruminate
Till all fears and doubts are gone
Be aware of your identity
And victory through the Son

Daddy's waiting
Every day
Just in case
You pass this way
You asked for your share
Of the inheritance
Spent it all
On song and dance
Women and wine
Tankards of beer
Was that such
A good idea?
You went to a farm
To look after pigs
Now you're eating their food
And sleeping on twigs
Now at last
You've come to your right mind
Return to Daddy
He was always kind
With fear and trembling
You walk down the road
A weight of guilt
You carry as a load
Daddy sees you
A precious sight
He throws his arms
Around you tight
The best robe in the house
And a ring for your finger
Loving eyes
Upon you linger
Daddy's waiting
For every child
Who's gone astray
Or just run wild

FROM THE DEPTHS OF MY TOMB

From the depths of my tomb
I heard His voice
Between death and life
I had a choice

I saw His light
Come shining in
To show I could
Walk free from sin

I heard Him say
Come follow me
Take off the grave clothes
And walk free

You may hear Him
Don't ignore
Like those times
You did before

Is anyone thirsty?
Is anyone thirsty
Is anyone yearning deep inside
Is anyone empty
The only thing stopping you is pride

Does anyone wake up
To another pointless day
Bury your head in the covers
That's where it will stay

Now there can be a change
It's easily arranged
Each day can be brand new
It sounds too good to be true

A life with meaning and joy
Like a child with a brand new toy
Wake up with a purpose
Instead of feeling morose

With Jesus life is exciting
All He needs is inviting
He's knocking at the door
Your life can be so much more

Open the door please don't wait
It's really not a matter of fate
Open the door let Him in
A new heart in you He will create

ALWAYS SINGING OVER YOU

God's always singing over you
He's singing with a love so true

His song will never ever end
He loves you more than your best friend

He never slumbers, never sleeps
He hears you in those times you weep

You're number one in His top hits
That is amazing, you must admit

Created to be His special treasure
For you His love is without measure

When troubles come
As oft they will
He calls to my storm
"Peace, be still!"

When fears assail
My troubled mind
I have a Saviour
Loving and kind

He understands
My frail frame
In fact He even
Calls me by name

When through deep waters
I chance to travel
I won't be overcome
In this I marvel

He calls me precious
Calls me His child
Though I've done some things
That were quite wild

I'm forgiven and loved
Not for what I've done
But because of the sacrifice
Of God's own son

A beautiful garden
A sight to behold
I've heard all about it
In stories of old

Where God walked with man
In the cool of the day
And he simply listened
To what God had to say

Only one tree
From which not to eat
"Just trust in me children
And sit at my feet"

One day in the garden
A snake did appear
"Did God really say?"
He hissed with a sneer

"Eat of that tree
You won't need him at all
You'll be wise like him
And you'll have a ball"

They gave in to that tempter
One fateful bite they took
All innocence was gone
Now fearfully they looked

Hiding in the bushes
When God walked that way
They were feeling guilty
On that fateful day

Fig leaves for clothes
God saw their sorry state
"Who told you that you're naked?"
Forbidden fruit has sealed your fate

God lovingly supplied
Clothing made of skins
Took them from the garden
Where sin had entered in

He couldn't let them eat
Of the tree of life
Or forever they would live
He limited their strife

In His heart He knew
A remedy would come
It would cost Him everything
The life of His own son

I have a dream
To see the lost get saved
To see the dead be raised

To see the church get bold
As in the days of old

Get back to the time of Acts
We can't deny the facts

Of Holy Spirit power
Climb down from ivory towers

Get back to our vision
Fulfil the great commission

Preach like Wesley on his horse
History can change it's course

A revival taking place
This time it's of grace

To see unity not strife
Dry bones come to life

You're dressing up the Christmas tree
With lights so bright and gay
To try and hide the empty space
That's growing every day

You're wrapping up the presents
As you hide behind the mask
You're formulating answers
To the questions that they'll ask

How are you today dear?
You're so good at pretending
That everything is fine
That you've had a happy ending

The smile you wear is fake
So no one ever knows
The pain you feel inside
The emptiness that grows

You try to fill the space
With things that should bring pleasure
But there's always something missing
That elusive buried treasure

I remember one like you
One who hunted high and low
Lookng for some happiness
Searching to and fro

I found my source of happiness
He filled the void within
I found a loving Saviour
He took away my sin

True happiness is found
Not in things external
But in the Saviour's love
His love is eternal

This building won't be shaken
This building won't be moved
It's built on firm foundation
Which cannot be improved

Built on not just words
But built on actions too
As we advance His Kingdom
With love that's strong and true

When stormy gales arrive
We will fear no fear
With Jesus at the centre
They're sure to disappear

Now we as living stones
With love as the mortar
And Holy Spirit power
This world we can alter

We reinforce His reign
As Jesus went ahead
We'll follow in His footsteps
And even raise the dead.

Let's change the world together
As we build in unity
With Jesus as the cornerstone
As it's meant to be

Does God live in the sky?

Does God live in the sky
Does He have a long white beard
When you think of seeing Him
Does it fill your heart with fear

The enemy has lied
And told us that he's stern
Waiting to beat us up
If we do things out of turn

God isn't mad with you
He gave His only son
His finished work can bring you close
It's already done!

All the wrath and anger
Was poured out on the cross
Sin and death are beaten now
The enemy has lost

Still he'll try to bring his lies
When condemnation comes
To distance us from Father
He'll beat the same old drum

If we renew our minds
To the truth of God's word
We'll realise it's all hot air
And be free as a bird

We'll fly into our fathers arms
Without hesitation
Thanking Him every minute
For perfect salvation

I love to watch the clouds
As they are passing by
That one there's an island
Where palm trees reach the sky

A pirate ship is sailing
On the sea so blue
Captain Hook is waiting
For a crocodile or two

Pure white sand is calling
It seems to know my name
In my imagination
The island's glad I came

Relax upon the beach
With coconuts to eat
I'm sure that know
This really is a treat

I'm wearing a grass skirt
Flowers in my hair
And no one here in sight
Who can stop and stare

Another summer day

Another summer day
But what to do, not sure
Maybe we'll go swimming
And walk across Hob moor
With sandwiches and cakes
To eat along the way
Walking through the long grass
As trees gently sway
Are you sure there are no snakes?
Those cows look like they'll chase us
Eating our lunch
Feeling quite nervous
Edmund Wilson baths
We laughed and chased and played
We really could have stayed there
For days and days and days
Childhood goes so fast
Why does time have to hurry?
I'll hold it in my memories
For years to come, don't worry

April Fool's day

It's April fool's day
Hip hip hooray
Their dad had hatched a naughty plan
To wake those girls, fast as He can
Fire! Fire! He called, and knocked on every door
Those girls woke up, ran outside
Of fire, they were sure
Just dressing gowns and slippers
As they stood outside and shivered
Looking for the flames
Their bodies shook and quivered.
Then Dad popped out, big smile on his face
It's April fool's day!
what disgrace!
We ran inside and laughed with glee
Our house was safe, even the tree!
We had to laugh with rascally dad
He really was such a card
Just wait till next year, we'll plot a plan
To get our revenge on that naughty man

Christmas at Grandads

Out come the party dresses
Spending an eternity curling flowing tresses
Christine had a purple one and was Tracy's brown?
Rachel a Victorian dress
It was the best in town
We all pile in the car
And drive to Grandads' house
The area so quiet
You can even hear a mouse
Vera's cooked a turkey and a Christmas pud
She really has excelled this year
We have to listen to the Queen's speech
It really is quite boring
And grandad had some brandy
So now he's started snoring!
Time for entertainment!
The violin comes out
Rachel looking studious
Posing with a pout
Jenny has a tantrum
Grandad gets quite cross
Puts her in the hallway
Well, he is the boss
Tracy plays the cornet
You know she is quite good
Grandad filming all the fun
Good times he understood
Happy family memories
Will never go away
Grandad may be gone now
But in our memories, he'll stay

ESMERALDA

Esmerelda was a wonderful car
She was a sight to behold
1.8 Granada
Her colour it was gold

She took us to the seaside
To play down on the beach
She took us places near and far
Nowhere was out of reach

We didn't have to push her
Up that long steep hill
She left all other cars
At a stand still

Why did she get that name?
I really do not know
But every week Dad polished her
His love for her to show

She really was his pride and joy
To carry folks around
He was proud to drive her
When he went into town

We made some special memories
I never will forget
Of sunny days and picnics
Of that there are no regrets

She'll always have a special place
In this heart of mine
Our beloved Esmerelda
Made some special times

GARROWBY HILL

Garrowby hill, at 2 in the morning
Its early still, light is not dawning
It might be Russia or further tonight
CB radio clutched so tight
4 in the morning Stayed up all night
Household fast asleep Eyes closed tight
Radio mast seems to reach to the sky
Sideband radio, me oh my
Postcard drops through the door

Face excited, this is what it was for!
Signal strength and location
Serious stuff, not a vacation
! What is this fuss all about I wonder
Those crazy plans I often ponder
Head in the clouds, a dreamer at heart
Stretch limousines, how did it all start?
We were just bits of kids That didn't have a clue
Muddling by in life It was the best that we could do
Be sure we both loved you all Though we made mistakes
If it was a movie We could have another take
I wouldn't change those times Though they were really tough
Sometimes it has to be that way We have to learn from stuff
Looking back with laughter Is what it's all about
Thinking of the happy times They were plenty, there's no doubt.

Fond Memories

I have some fond memories
When children played at my feet
Some are not so happy
Some are really sweet
Life was tough at times
Money was really scarce
I got adept at bargain hunting
On Fridays I would race
To the fish stall on the market
At the end of the day
Small pieces of fish to buy
A small price I could pay
See their faces all aglow
Home made chips and fish
Every Friday evening
Our favourite dish

Mums's Visit

It Took all day to hoover and dust
To get that house clean
Really was a must
The windows are gleaming
Not one spot in sight
Beds made neatly
Now breath held tight
Mum's coming to visit
Her eyes are like hawks
Children must be well behaved
Not even just one squawk
All seems to go well
Till it's time to leave
Eagle eyes spot the garden
My stomach starts to heave
"Pick a weed as you go!"
Oh why did she see
The one thing that I didn't do
She seemed to speak with glee
It didn't matter
All the hours I laboured and I toiled
Just one simple weed
Had all my efforts spoiled

My Dining room

My dining room was a really special place
Somewhere to hide under the table
Somewhere to slide on socks, how unstable!
A tent, how exciting, with sheets, how inviting!
Sail across the sea in a cardboard box
A Dalek in a basket , be careful of those rocks!
A racing track for cars to see whose is the fastest
A dressing up contest, how fantastic
Summer holidays, rainy days
Spent in many happy ways

The doors are always open

The doors are always open
But today they're closed
Whatever could have happened?
Do you suppose?
Spent all morning getting ready
Braiding hair and curling tresses
The girls have to be pretty
In their Sunday dresses.
Usually a friendly smile
Is waiting at the door
Vigorous handshakes
For rich and for poor.
We quietly open
The door peek within
No sign of a soul
In the main hall, all dim.
But then comes a voice "Joyce where have you been?"
We thought you were ill
You haven't been seen.
Then like a light bulb just realised
The clocks had gone forward
I blushed, quite surprised.
Oh how we laughed and joked on that day
With friends that we cherished
And so it will stay.

Waking up
Early morning
Open the curtains
As day is dawning
A beautiful sight
Is there to behold
A story not written
It has not been told
There is a bite in the ait,
Frost on the ground
Crisp leaves underfoot,
Is the one and only sound
The artist has painted
Shades of purple and blue
A thin mist rises
From the morning dew
A low sun appears
To kiss the clouds
Out here in the fields
Where there are no crowds

My favourite place to be

Printed in Great Britain
by Amazon

32128415R00044